Henry's House

WALDEN
POND

Southeast
Corner

N

Scale in feet

0 250 500

IF YOU SPENT A DAY WITH THOREAU AT WALDEN POND

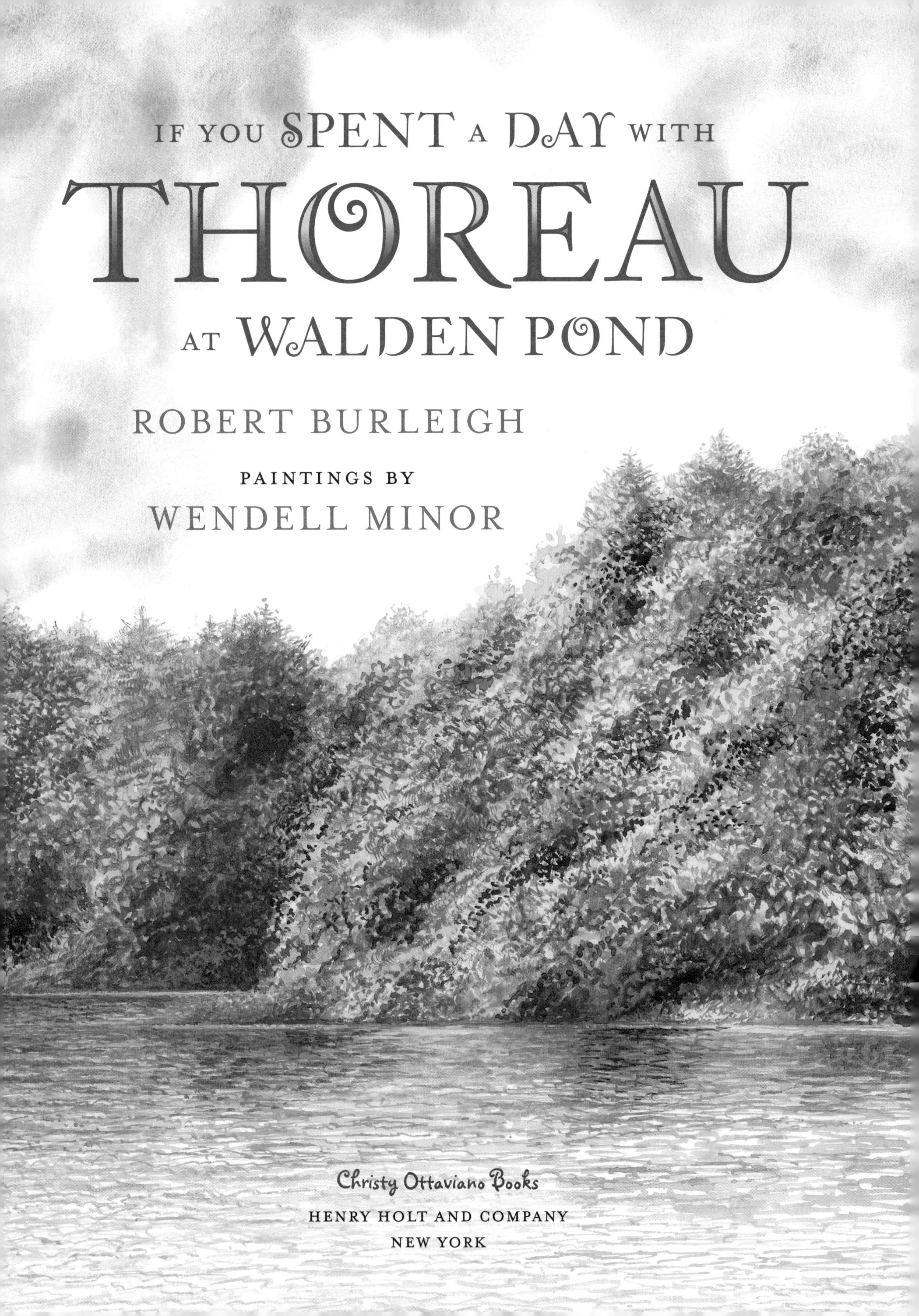

IF YOU SPENT A DAY WITH THOREAU AT WALDEN POND

ROBERT BURLEIGH

PAINTINGS BY
WENDELL MINOR

Christy Ottaviano Books
HENRY HOLT AND COMPANY
NEW YORK

If you spent a day with Henry David Thoreau, you would need to get there early because Henry wakes with the sun.

If you spent a day with Henry David Thoreau, you would knock on the door of Henry's tiny house on the shore of Walden Pond. Hello, Henry!

You would look inside and see nothing but three chairs, a table, a desk, and an old bed. Yet Henry has just what he needs.

If you spent a day with Henry David Thoreau, you would sit on the soft pine needles behind the house and drink cold, fresh Walden water. "Living a simple life is the best way to be happy," says Henry.

You would row out onto the pond, gaze down deep, and glimpse a beautiful gold and emerald fish. *Swish!* It's gone!

You would help Henry weed his bean patch. "I like to make the earth say 'beans' instead of 'grass,'" Henry says with a grin.

If you spent a day with Henry David Thoreau, you would head down paths that wind back and forth through leafy woods. But Henry knows the way.

You would sometimes stop and listen. "Shhhhh," Henry says, holding a finger to his lips. "That's a robin calling to his friends. And that gentle song is the coo of a mourning dove, and there's the screech of an angry jay."

If you spent a day with Henry David Thoreau, you would wade in Sandy Pond and let the cool water lap against your feet and feel the sun on the back of your neck.

You would point to a hawk high above,
soaring and tumbling, over and over.

“So wild and free,” says Henry. (And he writes it down in his notebook, too.)

If you spent a day with Henry David Thoreau, you would hike past Fair Haven Hill, where the huckleberries grow, pick the ripest ones, and nibble them as you roamed. Yum!

You would spy from your hiding place a mother partridge shooing her chicks under dry leaves. See them?

Look at their tiny brown eyes staring out!

If you spent a day with Henry David Thoreau, you would climb a farmer's fence, shortcut across a pasture, and call out to the cows.

You would rest on the grass, lean back, hear the leaves murmur, and feel the soft breeze against your face. Henry calls it "dreaming awake."

If you spent a day with Henry, you would share a loaf of his homemade bread. After lunch, you would feed bits of cheese to a tiny mouse and laugh as its whiskers tickled your hand.

You would follow a fox across the meadow—running far behind it, losing the track but finding it again and again. "Be quick!" says Henry.

You would lie on the ground, staring down, watching an ant war—red versus black. To Henry, little things matter as much as big things.

If you spent a day with Henry David Thoreau, you would relax together watching. Late-afternoon clouds seem to float on Walden Pond.

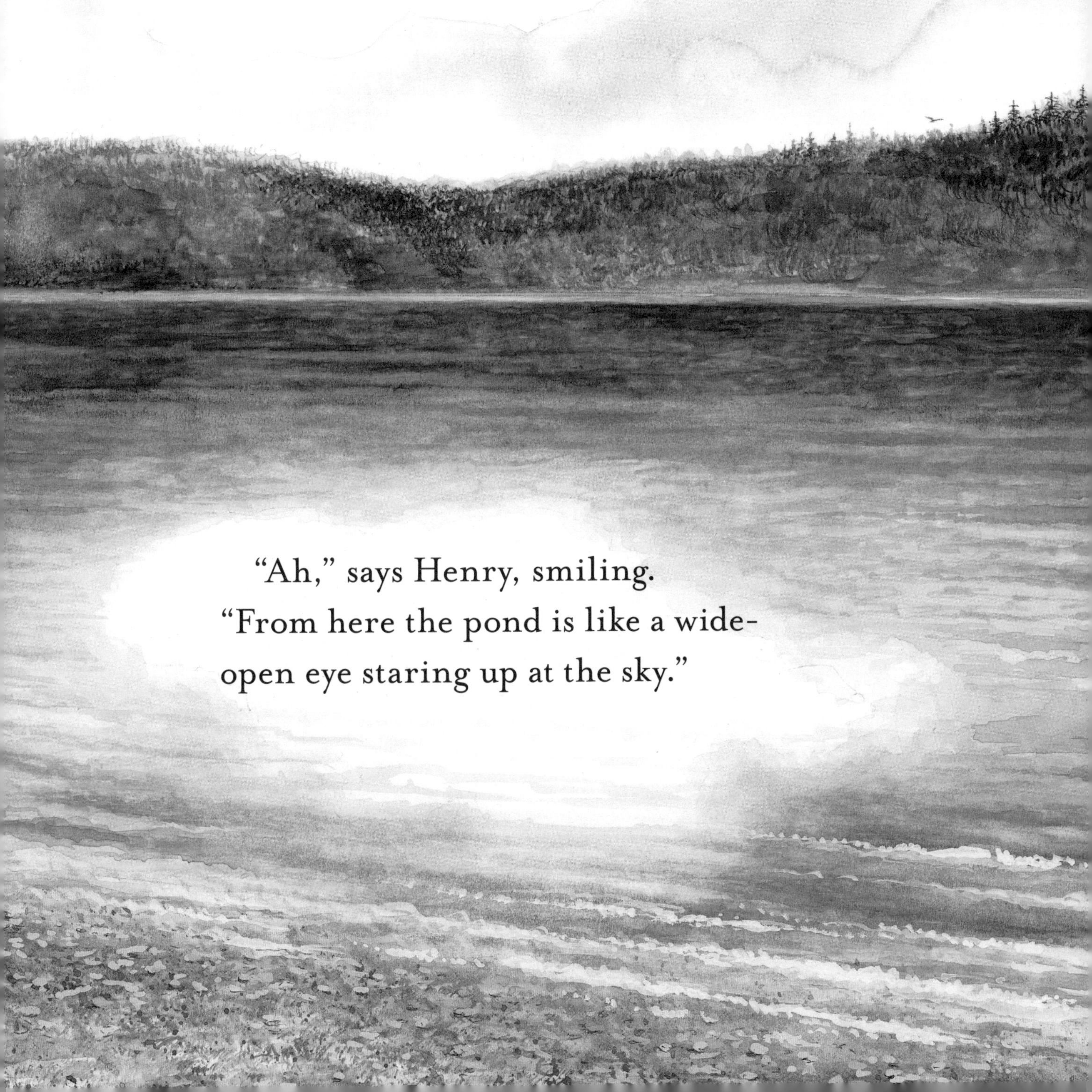

"Ah," says Henry, smiling. "From here the pond is like a wide-open eye staring up at the sky."

If you spent a day with Henry David Thoreau, when you left, you would glance back in the gathering dusk and wave.

You would see Henry writing in his journal by the light of his kerosene lamp. He would look up and call, "Remember—have an adventure every day!"

"Good-bye, Henry, and thanks!" you would call back with a happy smile—if you spent a day with Henry David Thoreau.

More Things to Know About
HENRY DAVID THOREAU

HENRY DAVID THOREAU was born in 1817 and died in 1862. He lived most of his life in and around Concord, Massachusetts.

His most famous book is called *Walden.* It tells why he went to the woods and what he did and learned during the two years he lived there.

He also kept a daily journal, noting the many things he saw and thought.

He went for long walks almost every day, even in winter.

He said he left his house by Walden Pond because he "had several more lives to live and could not spare any more time for that one."

The materials for Thoreau's house cost just $28.12! (This is about $800 in today's money.)

Henry never married. But even though he loved his solitude, he also loved dancing, ice skating, and discussing ideas with his many friends.

Thoreau sometimes disagreed with the policy of the American government. He was strongly opposed to the Mexican War in 1848 and to slavery.

Thoreau believed people should follow their dreams. He once wrote, "If a man does not keep pace with his companions, perhaps it is because he hears a different drummer. Let him step to the music which he hears, however measured and far away."

When he died in 1862, few people had read his books or even knew his name. But today Henry David Thoreau is read and loved by people all over the world.

The Thoreau Society is dedicated to celebrating and circulating Thoreau's ideas and writings. Founded in 1941, the society sponsors many Thoreau-related publications and events. You can write them for more information at info@thoreausociety.org or at 341 Virginia Road, Concord, MA 01742.

Observations by Thoreau

HENRY DAVID THOREAU wrote or said many things that people still read and remember because his words seem beautiful and true. Of course, he was writing over 150 years ago, so his language can sometimes be difficult to understand today.

Here are some of Thoreau's thoughts with modern interpretations:

"If you have built castles in the air . . . put the foundations under them."

If you have dreams, work hard to make them come true.

"Our houses are such unwieldy property that we are often imprisoned rather than housed in them."

Thoreau thought that we often pay so much money and use up so much time in keeping up our houses that they are more like burdens, or prisons, instead of being pleasant places in which to live.

"That man is the richest whose pleasures are the cheapest."

To live simply and cheaply makes a person most happy, and in a sense, most rich.

"It is never too late to give up our prejudices."

No matter how old you are, you can still change your old ideas for better, truer ones.

"Our life is frittered away by detail. . . . Simplify, simplify."

People get exhausted by dealing with small things. But they could get rid of these many details if they tried to make their lives more simple.

"How many a man has dated a new era in his life from the reading of a book!"

Reading a book that means a lot to you can change your life.

"Heaven is under our feet as well as over our heads."

The best things in life can be nearby, and not always far off.

"In wildness is the preservation of the world."

Going back to nature will always make you and the world better.

"If a man does not keep pace with his companions, perhaps it is because he hears a different drummer. Let him step to the music which he hears."

People are not the same, and they will find truth and beauty by following their own ways.

"I love the wild not less than the good."

Thoreau loves the wilderness and the spirit of freedom it represents as much as he loves being a good person.

For Tom and Mary Jo Galetto
—R. B.

To the memory of my dear friend, Jean Craighead George,
who brought nature to generations of children in
the spirit of Henry David Thoreau
—W. M.

Henry Holt and Company, LLC
Publishers since 1866
175 Fifth Avenue
New York, New York 10010
mackids.com

Library of Congress Cataloging-in-Publication Data
Burleigh, Robert.
If you spent a day with Thoreau at Walden Pond / Robert Burleigh ;
illustrations by Wendell Minor. — 1st ed.
p. cm.
ISBN 978-0-8050-9137-3 (hc)
1. Thoreau, Henry David, 1817–1862—Juvenile literature. I. Minor, Wendell, ill. II. Title.
PS3053.B78 2012 818'.309—dc23 2011034306

First Edition—2012 / Designed by April Ward
The artist used gouache watercolor on Strathmore 500 Bristol paper
to create the illustrations for this book.

Printed in China by South China Printing Co. Ltd.,
Dongguan City, Guangdong Province
1 3 5 7 9 10 8 6 4 2

Site of Henry's House
Wyman
Meadow
Thoreau's
Cove
Ice Fort
Cove
Little
Cove
Deep
Cove